STO

Young Melvin
and Bulger

Also by Mark Taylor

HENRY THE EXPLORER

HENRY EXPLORES THE JUNGLE

HENRY THE CASTAWAY

HENRY EXPLORES THE MOUNTAINS

THE BOLD FISHERMAN

A TIME FOR FLOWERS

THE OLD WOMAN AND THE PEDLAR

OLD BLUE, YOU GOOD DOG YOU!

BOBBY SHAFTO'S GONE TO SEA

THE FISHERMAN AND THE GOBLET

LAMB, SAID THE LION, I AM HERE

THE WIND'S CHILD

JENNIE JENKINS

TIME FOR OLD MAGIC
(BY MAY HILL ARBUTHNOT AND MARK TAYLOR)

TIME FOR NEW MAGIC
(BY MAY HILL ARBUTHNOT AND MARK TAYLOR)

THE SECRET LIFE OF ANGUS MC ANGUS

GOD, I LISTENED: THE LIFE OF EULA MC CLANEY
(BY EULA MC CLANEY AND MARK TAYLOR)

Young Melvin

illustrated by Jan Brett

and Bulger

by MARK TAYLOR

DOUBLEDAY & COMPANY, INC.
GARDEN CITY, NEW YORK

Adapted from GOD BLESS THE DEVIL!:
LIARS' BENCH TALES, edited by James
R. Aswell. Copyright 1940 The University of
North Carolina Press. By permission of the
publisher.

Library of Congress Catalog Card Number 79-7118
ISBN: 0-385-15190-X Trade
ISBN: 0-385-15191-8 Prebound
Copyright © 1981 by MARK TAYLOR
All Rights Reserved
Printed in the United States of America

First Edition

Young Melvin and Bulger

Ever hear of Young Melvin?

He lived way up at the forks of Rocky Creek. He was called Young Melvin on account of his pappy was called Old Melvin. But Old Melvin died one day. That left Young Melvin all by himself—except for his hound dog named Bulger.

It was mighty lonely for the two of 'em. Bulger just got sort of droopy, and Young Melvin sat around feelin' low-down about things. Without Old Melvin to holler at 'em and make 'em take notice, there wasn't much for 'em to do. The crops had all dried up. The cow had been sold. The horse had run off. And all the chickens had disappeared one night—like as not when a fox family came and got 'em while Young Melvin and Bulger was both sleepin'.

But it could have been worse. Young Melvin and Bulger still had each other. And Young Melvin also had some money put by in his granny's old butter crock that was hid in the broken-down wagon that was out in the cow shed that was half-settled into the marshy field where the creek liked to run over in the spring and summer and fall when it rained.

Young Melvin got to thinkin' about the world. He hadn't ever seen it. He hadn't ever been further from home than to go down to the settlement over at the crossroads. And it come to Young Melvin's mind that now was as good a time as ever to go see what the world was like. After that, he could come back home and figure out what to do about him and Bulger.

So Young Melvin put out the fire, buried the butter crock under the sycamore, shut up the house, and started off with Bulger. He kept goin' 'til he got to the crossroads.

Old Bulger couldn't hardly believe all them houses and all them people could be in one place, and all them smells that went with 'em just set his nose a-twitchin'. But Young Melvin didn't stop to jaw with no one, and he didn't let Bulger stop neither. He just went straight to Mister Old Man Bill Blowdy's house. That's how Young Melvin was. When there was one thing on his mind, there wasn't no other thing on it at all.

Mister Old Man Bill Blowdy used to know Young Melvin's pappy. His pappy always said what a sharp old cuss Mister Old Man Bill Blowdy was. That old man didn't look so sharp—least not to Young Melvin. He was big and fat, all red in the face, and always grinnin' and talkin' like he had a mouthful of honey. But he was always beatin' somebody in a deal or settin' the law on 'em. 'Cause all Mister Old Man Bill Blowdy thought about was gettin' the best of other folks and makin' money. Why, he'd even got the best of Old Melvin more than once, and Young Melvin had promised his pappy never to forget it.

Now Mister Old Man Bill Blowdy happened to be lookin' out his window, like he was always doin', to see was any troublesome man, woman, or child comin' to bother him. When he saw Young Melvin makin' straight for the house, with Bulger sort of trailin' behind, he just

figured Young Melvin was comin' to ask him a favor. So he scrambled to and locked the door and hunkered down in his chair and out of sight.

Young Melvin come up on the porch and pounded on the door. His pappy used to say the only way to get Mister Old Man Bill Blowdy to open the door was to start knockin' it down. Young Melvin pounded and pounded, but he couldn't rouse Mister Old Man Bill Blowdy. So then Young Melvin looked through the window, and there was the old man's feet stickin' out on the floor with the rest of him hunkered down in the chair.

"He's just sittin' there asleep," Young Melvin said to Bulger. "We got to rouse him."

So Young Melvin began poundin' louder than before, and Bulger started scratchin', and it looked like that door wasn't goin' to last much longer.

"Mister Old Man Bill Blowdy!" hollered Young Melvin. "Wake up! Wake up!"

At last Mister Old Man Bill Blowdy come to the door and opened it a crack. "Who's there?" he said, like he didn't know.

"It's me, Young Melvin," said Young Melvin.

"Oh, Young Melvin, so it is," said Mister Old Man Bill Blowdy. Then that old man sighed as if he were breathin' his very last breath. "I'm feelin' pretty tired and sick and all fidgety in my limbs, and tryin' awful hard to get some rest so as to linger a bit longer in this hard old world. But I suppose you was expectin' to be asked in?"

"No use to come in," said Young Melvin, "'cause I'd just be comin' right back out."

"That's mighty sensible," said Mister Old Man Bill Blowdy, gettin' ready to shut the door. "It was nice of you to stop by, Young Melvin."

"Wait," said Young Melvin. "I stopped by for a reason."

Mister Old Man Bill Blowdy didn't look too pleased to hear it. "You did?" he said, kind of suspicious.

"Yes, sir," said Young Melvin. "You see, I'm on my way to town! It's forty miles and clear across this county, and the next, and the next one after that. But I'm on my way! That's why I come here to see you."

Well, that made Mister Old Man Bill Blowdy look like he'd just heard some bad news. "Now listen here, Young Melvin," he said, startin' once more to shut the door, "I'm pretty hard up for money just now. Hard up, and feelin' poorly, and just all done in."

"But I didn't come to ask for money," said Young Melvin. He'd stuck his foot in the door, so Mister Old Man Bill Blowdy couldn't get it shut.

"You don't want no money?" said Mister Old Man Bill Blowdy, like he just couldn't believe it.

"No, sir," said Young Melvin.

"And you don't want to make some kind of deal?" said Mister Old Man Bill Blowdy, like he wasn't hearin' right.

"No, sir," said Young Melvin.

Then Mister Old Man Bill Blowdy just stood there not knowin' what to say. All he knew was makin' deals and tryin' to get the best of folks. That's what life was all about.

"I'm here to ask a favor of you," said Young Melvin.

Well, that did it. "I should've knowed!" Mister Old Man Bill Blowdy declared. The word "favor" just made him fit to spit nails. He hated that word. His red face went pale, and his heart began hammerin', and his hands set to shakin'. "A *favor*!" he shouted. "I never do no favors for nobody—not now nor never, not no time nohow!"

"But it's a favor I'm aimin' to pay for," said Young Melvin.

Mister Old Man Bill Blowdy got peaceful all of a sudden. "To *pay* for? he said all quiet and slow.

"Yes, sir," said Young Melvin.

"Oh, that's a different story," said Mister Old Man Bill Blowdy, like the taste of somethin' sweet was on his tongue. He give Young Melvin a sly grin, and the color come back to his face. "What's this here favor you want to *pay* me for?"

"I want you to keep my hound dog, Bulger, for me while I'm gone," said Young Melvin. "I figure you wouldn't let no harm come to him."

"How do you figure that?" said Mister Old Man Bill Blowdy.

"Well, Pappy always said you kept a sharp eye on things and not even a hound dog could get a scent on you," said Young Melvin.

"And your pappy was right," said Mister Old Man Bill Blowdy.

"Will you keep Bulger for me?" asked Young Melvin. "I don't know when I'll be back. It's across two counties to town, and I aim to look things over pretty good. But I'll be back next week, or next month, or sometime."

"Oh, you just take your time," said Mister Old Man Bill Blowdy. "I'll watch over Bulger like he was my own kin."

Now Mister Old Man Bill Blowdy didn't have no kin, leastwise none that wanted to own up they was kin to him. And he thought kinfolk were the worst kind of folk, 'cause they was the ones that were always expectin' *favors.* But that old man had him a scheme in his mind, a scheme to get him some money and a good old hound dog, too. He could tell, just by lookin' at him, that Young Melvin wasn't too bright.

So Young Melvin said good-bye to Bulger. They both looked awful sad. Of course, Bulger always had tears in

17

his old red eyes, but by the time they said "good-bye" and
"be good," Young Melvin's eyes was full of tears, too, and
just as red as Bulger's.

"Now come along!" said Mister Old Man Bill Blowdy,
kind of impatient. "I've just about used up my strength for
one day, and you got to get started on to town, Young
Melvin."

"Wait for me 'til I get back!" called Young Melvin, as he
started on down the Long Road.

"Oh, just don't you worry!" called Mister Old Man Bill
Blowdy. "You take all the time you want."

Well, Young Melvin crossed two counties and on into
the next. It was a longer walk than he'd counted on, seein'
as how he had to ford several creeks and a pretty broad
river, and hike up and down some big hills, and work his
way through a swamp or two, climb over a whole string of
mountains, and push through some woods where he kept
gettin' lost. But folks were friendly enough, once they
decided he wasn't just some robber or idle vagrant. Why,
they'd call off their dogs, put down their shotguns, and
even let him sleep in the barn—especially if he paid 'em
somethin' or did some work. And once he met a kindly old
lady that let him stay overnight for nothin'—give him a
good bed and a tasty meal. So Young Melvin sat up late
and shared all the news with her about his pappy, and
Bulger, and Mister Old Man Bill Blowdy.

When Young Melvin finally come to town, he was so
amazed by the sights he couldn't hardly think they was
real at first. He hadn't never imagined such *fine* places—
fancy stores, and big houses painted bright colors, and
eatin' places where you could eat just about anything you
wanted. And when he saw the *fine* buggies pulled by the
fine, smart-prancin' horses, and the hotel with all them
rooms and people just comin' and goin' so *fine* and easy, he

thought it must be like heaven. Only why would anyone want to go to heaven when they could just come to town?

Young Melvin wandered all about and took his time lookin' at the sights. He stayed in a boardin' house for only fifty cents a day, with a fancy room he shared with three important gentlemen, and with all the most wonderful food he could eat. And after the folks in town knew he had enough money to pay for things, they was just as agreeable as they could be. But Young Melvin knew better than to spend his money on high livin'. "I'm keepin' the most of it for a rainy day," he'd say. And wasn't it lucky for him that it didn't rain even once while he was there!

So at last Young Melvin had seen all there was to see. Of course, he could've gone on and seen more of the world, but he said to himself, "I'd better go on home and rest up, and get some more money out of the butter crock, and let Bulger know I'm all right, and then maybe I'll strike out for other parts."

Soon after that, Young Melvin turned up at the crossroads. He'd been gone more than a month, and the trip back home took longer than the trip to town, 'cause it rained all the way. But there he come, limpin' down the Long Road, covered with mud, but lookin' real easy in his mind. And, of course, Mister Old Man Bill Blowdy was lookin' out the window as usual and saw Young Melvin makin' straight for his house. Well, that old man knew what to do—just sat tight in his chair and waited.

Young Melvin come up on the porch and started poundin' on the door and hollerin', "I'm back, Mister Old Man Bill Blowdy!"

"Who's back?" called Mister Old Man Bill Blowdy.

"Me, Young Melvin, that's who!" shouted Young Melvin.

23

Mister Old Man Bill Blowdy come to the door and opened it a crack—not so big as Young Melvin could get his foot in it—and said, "Well, well! How are you, Young Melvin?"

"I'm just right," said Young Melvin, "considerin' where I've been and what I've seen. I've been to town and back, across three counties, twice times forty miles, over creeks and rivers, hills and mountains, through valleys, swamps, and darksome woods, and I'm back."

"Glad to hear it," said Mister Old Man Bill Blowdy, startin' to shut the door. "Next time you get to the crossroads, stop by and say hello."

"Hold on!" said Young Melvin.

"I'm busy," said Mister Old Man Bill Blowdy.

But somehow Young Melvin got his foot in the door. "Where's Bulger, Mister Old Man Bill Blowdy?"

"Who?" said Mister Old Man Bill Blowdy, tryin' to shut the door.

"My foxhound!" said Young Melvin. "You know— Bulger."

"Oh, *him!*" said Mister Old Man Bill Blowdy. "Why, I'd nearly forgot all about him."

"How could you forget about him, when you got him?" said Young Melvin.

"That's just it," said Mister Old Man Bill Blowdy, lookin' real sorry. "I wouldn't never forget him, if I had him. But since I don't have him, why, I reckon it's easy enough to forget him—if you follow what I'm sayin'."

"I don't follow it one little bit," said Young Melvin. "Where's my hound dog?"

"Well, he's all gone, Young Melvin," said Mister Old Man Bill Blowdy.

"All gone?" said Young Melvin. "How can a hound dog be all gone?"

"That's a good question, Young Melvin," said Mister Old Man Bill Blowdy. "'Cause I didn't say he was gone away. I said he was all gone, 'cause that's what he is—all gone. Darnedest thing ever happened to a hound dog that I ever heard of. I hardly like to talk about it."

"Well, I wish you would," said Young Melvin. And it looked like he was goin' to get pretty mad.

"Well, then, I'll tell you, although it upsets me some to do it," said Mister Old Man Bill Blowdy. "I don't much like to talk about such things as happened to that hound dog.

"You see, after you was gone for about a week, I thought maybe Bulger'd be happy in that little tumbly-down house over in the Old Ground. My last renters had left it pretty dirty. Fact is, Young Melvin, they left it just a-crawlin' with chinchy bugs. Course, I didn't know that. But it seems them chinchy bugs was powerful hungry, what with nothin' around to eat for a long time. So they just ate up Bulger that very first night! Why, they even ate up the poor thing's bones—somethin' I never heard of before or since. All that was left was Bulger's old collar, and it was pretty well chewed on, too."

Mister Old Man Bill Blowdy stopped to sigh and to see how Young Melvin was takin' it. And when he saw the tears comin' to Young Melvin's eyes, he knew he had him. Truth was, he had Bulger hid away and plannin' to sell him to a man he knew over in the next county.

"Well, Young Melvin, I feel pretty bad about what happened," said the old man. "It ain't right for chinchy bugs to eat up a hound dog. But I aim to do what's right by you. So I won't charge you more 'n five dollars for keepin' Bulger that first week. After all, it was my fault to put him over there. And I won't charge you a penny for the valuable time I've lost worryin' over it."

26

Mister Old Man Bill Blowdy sighed like he was the sorriest man on earth and give Young Melvin a sly look. Well, Young Melvin looked bad, like he'd been squeezed by a bear, kicked by a mule, and stomped by a bull. His breath was just sort of all gone out of him. Then tears filled up his eyes, he dragged his sleeve across his nose, and he said, "Bulger was better than regular folks. Them chinchy bugs just don't know what they done to me."

"It's a pity," sniffled Mister Old Man Bill Blowdy. "I feel bad about it, too."

So Young Melvin gave Mister Old Man Bill Blowdy five dollars. Then he pulled his foot out of the door, took himself off the porch, and started across the road. Mister Old Man Bill Blowdy eased himself out the door to watch him go. It was just then Young Melvin turned around.

"Mister Old Man Bill Blowdy," said Young Melvin, "my place is way up the road, clear up to Rocky Creek. I'm tired after all my travels. And I'm low in my mind about Bulger. Could you lend me the use of your mule to ride home? I'll bring him back in the mornin'."

Now Mister Old Man Bill Blowdy knew that Young Melvin was as good as his word. And he was so pleased to think how he'd tricked the boy out of a good foxhound, and got five dollars from him as well, that he said, "Sure, Young Melvin, you just ride my old mule home and take the load off your feet."

So Mister Old Man Bill Blowdy got out the mule, a poorly lookin' critter that didn't seem fit for walkin', much less ridin'. Then he got Clancy to come over from the General Store across the road.

"Clancy, I want you to be witness to this loan," said Mister Old Man Bill Blowdy. "I'm lettin' Young Melvin here ride my mule home. He'll be bringin' him back in the mornin'."

28

Clancy laughed. "Well, I'll stand as witness. But I don't hardly suspect this mule can make it up to Young Melvin's place and back."

"He'd better," said Mister Old Man Bill Blowdy. "This here's my finest mule. I don't think Young Melvin's got money enough to pay for it, should anythin' happen to it."

But Young Melvin didn't answer back. He just got on the old mule and started for home. And it was hard to tell who was the sorrier sight—that old mule with its ribs stickin' out, or Young Melvin with his head bowed low.

The next mornin', Mister Old Man Bill Blowdy was up early. Just as soon as Young Melvin returned the mule, he was goin' to take Bulger from the hidin' place and ride over to the next county to deliver him. But the mornin' got later and later, and Young Melvin never showed up. And Mister Old Man Bill Blowdy began to worry. By the middle of the day, Young Melvin hadn't showed up yet, and Mister Old Man Bill Blowdy was so worried he began to feel sort of sick.

Well, late in the afternoon, Mister Old Man Bill Blowdy was gettin' ready to set the law on Young Melvin, when he saw him come walkin' down the road. But Young Melvin wasn't walkin' toward his house; he was walkin' toward the General Store. So Mister Old Man Bill Blowdy run out on his porch and hollered, "Hey, Young Melvin! Where's my mule?"

But Young Melvin just kept on walkin'. So Mister Old Man Bill Blowdy run after him and caught up to him on the steps of the General Store.

"Where's my mule, Young Melvin? Where's my mule?" the old man shouted.

"Who?" said Young Melvin.

"My mule!" shouted Mister Old Man Bill Blowdy.

"Oh, *him*," said Young Melvin. "Why, I'd nearly forgot all about him."

31

"How could you forget about my mule, when you got him?" said Mister Old Man Bill Blowdy, his face gettin' redder than usual.

"That's just it," said Young Melvin, lookin' real sorry. "I wouldn't never forget your mule, if I had him. But since I don't have him, why, I reckon it's easy enough to forget him—if you follow what I'm sayin'."

"You stop that!" shouted Mister Old Man Bill Blowdy. "Tell me what's done happened to my mule!"

Young Melvin shook his head slowly and said, "I feel mighty bad about that mule, Mister Old Man Bill Blowdy. But he's all gone."

"All gone!" screamed Mister Old Man Bill Blowdy. "How can a mule be all gone?"

"That's a good question, Mister Old Man Bill Blowdy," said Young Melvin. "'Cause I didn't say he was gone away, did I? I said he was all gone, 'cause that's what he is—all gone. Darnedest thing ever happened to a mule that I ever heard of. I hardly like to talk about it."

"Hold on there!" roared Mister Old Man Bill Blowdy, lookin' like he was about to blow to bits.

But Young Melvin just walked up the steps and into the General Store. Mister Old Man Bill Blowdy was so mad he ran across to Squire Rogers' house up the road a ways. Squire Rogers, that good old man, knew all about the law and how to settle things.

"Squire Rogers!" shouted Mister Old Man Bill Blowdy, just runnin' in without knockin'. "Young Melvin has done stole my best mule! I want you to handle him!"

"Wait just a minute," said Squire Rogers. "You only got one mule that I know of—if that's what you can call that poor critter. How you figure it's your *best* mule?"

"Don't ask me such questions now!" hollered Mister Old Man Bill Blowdy. "You got to do somethin' about Young Melvin."

"First things first," said Squire Rogers, that good old man. "Just tell me how you call only one mule the *best* mule."

"It's my best mule . . . 'cause . . . 'cause it's the best I could get," said Mister Old Man Bill Blowdy.

Squire Rogers looked at him and chuckled. "That's how I figured it, knowing how you like to get the most for the least."

"You lay off me, Squire!" said Mister Old Man Bill Blowdy. "It's Young Melvin you got to question."

So then Squire Rogers got his deputy to go and bring in Young Melvin. When the deputy come back with Young Melvin, everybody at the crossroads come taggin' along to see the excitement.

"Make him give me my mule or my money, and make him do it right now!" hollered Mister Old Man Bill Blowdy. He was turnin' redder and redder, like a fit was about to come on him.

"Now hold on, Bill Blowdy," said Squire Rogers, that good old man. "We do things fairly around here. I want everybody to sit down and keep quiet, while Young Melvin tells his side of things."

Then the Squire smiled at Young Melvin and said, "Young Melvin, they tell me you stole a mule."

"No, Squire, I never done such a thing," said Young Melvin.

Mister Old Man Bill Blowdy jumped up and shook his fist at Young Melvin. "You're a no-account, simple-minded, mule-stealin' liar!"

"You better quiet down, Bill Blowdy," said Squire Rogers. "Even though I've heard you know all about liars and lyin', I reckon we should let Young Melvin tell his side."

"He stole my mule, Squire," said Mister Old Man Bill Blowdy—nice and quiet. "That's my side. It's the only side."

"Son," said Squire Rogers to Young Melvin, "is that the only side to it?"

"No, Squire," said Young Melvin. "You see, I went a-travelin' and just got back yesterday. Mister Old Man Bill Blowdy there promised to look after my hound dog, Bulger, while I was gone—for pay. Well, when I come back yesterday, Mister Old Man Bill Blowdy told me how some chinchy bugs in his tumbly-down house over in the Old Ground done ate up Bulger—bones and all, in one night. I felt mighty bad about it. So I paid Mister Old Man Bill Blowdy five dollars for the week he had Bulger. And he was kind enough not to charge me for the trouble and worry he went through over Bulger and them chinchy bugs. So then I asked for the loan of his mule to ride home."

"My oh my!" said Squire Rogers. "The chinchy bugs are gettin' out of hand in this county."

"Well," said Young Melvin, "there I was, ridin' that mule up toward my place. It's a long ways, 'cause it's clear over the hill and way up to the forks of the creek. And I was just ridin' along, mindin' my own business and grievin' over Bulger, when all at once I saw a big old turkey buzzard droppin' down out of the sky. It was droppin' as fast as a hawk and crowin' like a rooster!

"Next thing I knowed, that buzzard just grabbed the mule by the tail and started back up in the sky. Well, the mule's hind legs lifted right off the ground, and I went flyin' over his head and hit a rock. It knocked me sort of senseless for a minute. When my mind cleared, there was that buzzard high in the sky, just a-sailin' away with Mister Old Man Bill Blowdy's mule."

Everybody drew in their breath at what Young Melvin was tellin', and Squire Rogers opened his eyes real wide.

"That's how it happened," said Young Melvin. "I sure am sorry about it, too."

"Hold on, son," said Squire Rogers, that good old man. "I've seen lots of turkey buzzards, but never one that could crow."

"That's because it's a lie!" shouted Mister Old Man Bill Blowdy, jumpin' up again and ready to come at Young Melvin. But the deputy held him down, and Squire Rogers fixed him with a good look.

"Squire, it surprised me some, too," said Young Melvin. "But then I got to thinkin' about it afterward. In a county where chinchy bugs can eat up a good old hound dog like Bulger in one night, I guess turkey buzzards can crow and carry off mules."

Everybody began laughin', 'cause they all knew the chinchy bugs was bad, but not that bad. So Squire Rogers agreed that if chinchy bugs could eat up foxhounds, turkey buzzards could carry off mules. And he said that one good lie surely deserved one back. And then it all come out how someone had seen Mister Old Man Bill Blowdy hide Bulger in another place. And someone else had heard Bulger bayin' and barkin' just the night before.

Squire Rogers, that good old man, made Mister Old Man Bill Blowdy give Bulger back to Young Melvin. And he made him give back the five dollars Young Melvin had paid—as punishment for lyin' to him. And he made him pay an extra five dollars for overchargin' Young Melvin in the first place. Then he made him pay Young Melvin five dollars for mistreatin' Bulger. And he made him pay ten dollars for cheatin' the man that was goin' to buy Bulger from him. Next he made him pay fifteen dollars for failin'

to tear down that tumbly-house full of chinchy bugs. And last, he made him pay a twenty-five dollar fine for tryin' to cheat Young Melvin in the first place. And all the money went to Young Melvin!

Then Young Melvin told Mister Old Man Bill Blowdy where he could find his mule. "It's just up at the foot of the hill," said Young Melvin. "The poor old thing couldn't carry me any further. It just sat down. And it was still sittin' there when I come by this afternoon. I guess you'll have to find a wagon to carry it home."

Mister Old Man Bill Blowdy was mocked and laughed at 'til he was forced to pay somebody to take a wagon and go fetch his mule. So altogether he was out a lot of money, and Young Melvin was the one that got it. So it seemed Young Melvin knew how to make a pretty good deal and wasn't so dumb after all.

Then Young Melvin told Squire Rogers that he suspected all along that Mister Old Man Bill Blowdy might try to cheat him, 'cause he used to cheat his pappy.

"I promised my pappy," said Young Melvin, "never to forget what Mister Old Man Bill Blowdy was like. And as for lettin' him look after Bulger? Well, Bulger would always find his way back to me—no matter what. Not even chinchy bugs would hinder him."

After that, Mister Old Man Bill Blowdy just sat in his house and fretted over how someone as simple as Young Melvin had outsmarted him. Some folks say he just grieved and pined away—that it wasn't no more than ten years before he took sick, wasted away, and died.

Well, that may be. As for Young Melvin and Bulger, they set off on more travels together. Young Melvin did enough farmin' to make more money to put in his granny's old butter crock. But every now and then he and Bulger

went off to see some of the world. And Young Melvin would tell stories to folks everywhere he went, about Mister Old Man Bill Blowdy, and Squire Rogers, that good old man, and all the folks at the crossroads, and all the strange things that *could* happen.

Did *you* ever hear about him?

MARK TAYLOR has written over a dozen trade books for young readers, including his award-winning Henry the Explorer books. Besides being a storyteller and balladeer, he has written numerous textbooks, television and film scripts, has his own television series for children, been a professor of children's literature, and worked as a children's and young adult librarian. Dr. Taylor currently devotes his time to writing, serving as an education consultant, and working in private practice as a counselor.

JAN BRETT wanted to become a children's book illustrator ever since she can remember, and *Young Melvin and Bulger* is now her fourth book. She draws and paints every day, but also manages to find time to pursue her other interests, which include riding and jumping horses, and flying sailplanes. She grew up and still lives in the seaside town of Hingham, Massachusetts, with her daughter, Lia.